W9-BTO-446

A Note to Parents and Caregivers:

With a focus on math, science, and social studies, *Read-it!* Readers support both the learning of content information and the extension of more complex reading skills. They encourage the development of problem-solving skills that help children expand their thinking.

 The PURPLE LEVEL presents basic topics and objects using high frequency words and simple language patterns.

 The RED LEVEL presents familiar topics using common words and repeating sentence patterns.

 The BLUE LEVEL presents new ideas using a larger vocabulary and varied sentence structure.

 The YELLOW LEVEL presents more challenging ideas, a broad vocabulary, and wide variety in sentence structure.

 The GREEN LEVEL presents more complex ideas, an extended vocabulary range, and expanded language structures.

 The ORANGE LEVEL presents a wide range of ideas and concepts using challenging vocabulary and complex language structures.

When sharing a content focused book with your child, read to find out facts and concepts, pausing often to restate and talk about the new information. The realistic story format provides an opportunity to talk about the language used, and to learn about reading to problem-solve for information. Encourage children to measure, make maps, and consider other situations that allow them to apply what they are learning.

There is no right or wrong way to share books with children. Find time to read and share new learning with your child, and pass on the legacy of literacy.

Adria F. Klein, Ph.D.
Professor Emeritus
California State University
San Bernardino, California

Editor: Shelly Lyons
Designer: Abbey Fitzgerald
Page Production: Michelle Biedscheid
Art Director: Nathan Gassman
Associate Managing Editor: Christianne Jones
The illustrations in this book were created with acrylics.

Picture Window Books
151 Good Counsel Drive
P.O. Box 669
Mankato, MN 56002-0669
877-845-8392
www.picturewindowbooks.com

Copyright © 2009 by Picture Window Books
All rights reserved. No part of this book may be reproduced without written
permission from the publisher. The publisher takes no responsibility for the use of
any of the materials or methods described in this book, nor for the products thereof.

Printed in the United States of America.

All books published by Picture Window Books
are manufactured with paper containing at least
10 percent post-consumer waste.

Library of Congress Cataloging-in-Publication Data
Emerson, Carl.
The cold winter day / by Carl Emerson ; iIllustrated by Cori Doerrfeld.
p. cm. — (Read-it! readers: Science)
ISBN 978-1-4048-2627-4 (library binding)
ISBN 978-1-4048-4758-3 (paperback)
1. Winter—Juvenile literature. I. Doerrfeld, Cori, ill. II. Title.
QB637.8.E44 2008
508.2—dc22   2008007166

The Cold Winter Day

by Carl Emerson
illustrated by Cori Doerrfeld

Special thanks to our advisers for their expertise:

Dr. Jon E. Ahlquist, Ph.D.
Department of Meteorology, Florida State University
Tallahassee, Florida

Adria F. Klein, Ph.D.
Professor Emeritus, California State University
San Bernardino, California

PICTURE WINDOW BOOKS
Minneapolis, Minnesota

Emma and Owen stepped off of the school bus.

The wind was cold against their faces.

The children looked at Old Oak.
"Old Oak looks cold," said Emma.

In North America, the winter season begins in December. It lasts until March. The seasons of spring, summer, and autumn follow.

Emma and Owen looked around the park. There were no people and no animals.

Some animals, like chipmunks, sleep during winter. Others, like some birds, fly south for the winter.

"Old Oak looks lonely," said Emma.

Emma and Owen walked home.

They talked about Old Oak.

11

"Old Oak must be sad," said Emma.

"She must be cold, too," Owen said.

Just then, Emma had an idea.

"We should help Old Oak warm up!"
said Emma.

The next morning, Emma and Owen
put on their winter clothes.

They carried a big box to the park.

During winter, the sun is at its lowest point in the sky. The number of daylight hours is less. Temperatures fall in most places, so the air feels cold.

"Hi, Old Oak!" Owen said.

"We have a surprise for you!"
said Emma.

Emma and Owen pulled hats, scarves, and mittens from the box.

They worked quickly to cover Old Oak's branches.

"There you go," Owen said.

"Now you will be warm," said Emma.

"Thank you," Old Oak said. "But the cold does not bother me."

During winter, most trees have no leaves. During summer, the trees store food inside their trunks. When winter arrives, the trees use the stored food to stay alive.

25

"I have another idea," Emma said.

"We will make you a friend."

Emma and Owen built a snowman.
They used two sticks for the arms.

Old Oak smiled. "It will be nice to have a friend for the winter," she said.

Fun Winter Activities

You can do many fun things in winter. Here are some ideas:

- Make your own icicles. Make a very small hole in a hanging container. Fill it with water and add a few drops of food coloring. Leave the container to slowly drip throughout a cold night. The next day, you will have a colored icicle.

- Put on warm clothing and head outside when it is snowing. Take a piece of black paper and a magnifying glass with you. Catch snowflakes on the black paper. Use the magnifying glass to look closely at each flake's special shape.

- Fold a large piece of white paper into four sections. Paint or draw four pictures of the same tree, showing how it looks in each season.

- String popcorn, cranberries, and nuts on a heavy string. Place it on a tree in your yard for a bird's winter feast.

Glossary

season—one of the four parts of the year; winter, spring, summer, and autumn
temperature—how hot or cold something is
winter—the season after autumn and before spring

To Learn More

More Books to Read

Castaldo, Nancy F. *Winter Day Play!* Chicago: Chicago Review Press, 2001.

Dixon, Ann. *Winter Is.* Portland, Ore.: Alaska Northwest Books, 2002.

Glaser, Linda. *It's Winter!* Brookfield, Conn.: Millbrook Press, 2002.

Roca, Núria. *Winter.* Hauppauge, N.Y.: Barron's Educational Series, 2004.

On the Web

FactHound offers a safe, fun way to find Web sites related to topics in this book. All of the sites on FactHound have been researched by our staff.

1. Visit *www.facthound.com*
2. Type in this special code: 1404826270
3. Click on the FETCH IT button.

Your trusty FactHound will fetch the best sites for you!

Look for all of the books in the *Read-it!* Readers: Science series:

Friends and Flowers (life science: bulbs)
The Grass Patch Project (life science: grass)
The Sunflower Farmer (life science: sunflowers)
Surprising Beans (life science: beans)

The Moving Carnival (physical science: motion)
A Secret Matter (physical science: matter)
A Stormy Surprise (physical science: electricity)
Up, Up in the Air (physical science: air)

The Autumn Leaf (Earth science: seasons)
The Busy Spring (Earth science: seasons)
The Cold Winter Day (Earth science: seasons)
The Summer Playground (Earth science: seasons)